PSC

UP!

by Kristine O'Connell George

Illustrated by Hiroe Nakata

Clarion Books · New York

Clarion Books
a Houghton Mifflin Company imprint
215 Park Avenue South, New York, NY 10003
Text copyright © 2005 by Kristine O'Connell George
Illustrations copyright © 2005 by Hiroe Nakata

The illustrations were executed in watercolor.
The text was set in 24-point Countryhouse and Smile ICG.

For information about permission to reproduce selections from this book, write to Permissions,
Houghton Mifflin Company, 215 Park Avenue South, New York, NY 10003.

www.houghtonmifflinbooks.com

Manufactured in China

Library of Congress Cataloging-in-Publication Data

George, Kristine O'Connell.
Up! / by Kristine O'Connell George ; illustrated by Hiroe Nakata.
p. cm.
Summary: Rhyming text and illustrations animate the feeling of "up"
as experienced by a little girl with her father.
ISBN 0-618-06489-3
[1. Senses and sensation—Fiction. 2. Fathers and daughters—Fiction.
3. Vocabulary. 4. Stories in rhyme.] I. Nakata, Hiroe, ill. II. Title.
PZ8.3.G2937Up 2005
[E]—dc22   2004010729

ISBN-13: 978-0-618-06489-2
ISBN-10: 0-618-06489-3

SCP   10 9 8 7 6 5 4 3 2

For the dads: Bill, Doug, Mike, Ray, and Rick.
In memory of their toddler-chasing days
—K.O.G.

For my father, who always wore
a red vest on Sundays
—H.N.

Up? Up!
The sun's up.
I'm up.
Is Daddy up?

Wake up, Daddy!
See me hopping.
Up. Up. Up!
Pigtails flopping.

Up the back
of the bouncy chair.
Boing. Boing!
Up in the air.

Lift me up!
A flying feeling.
I can almost
touch the ceiling.

Giddy up!
Grab Dad's ears.
Off to the park—
look who steers!

Climbing up,
walking tall.
Airplane arms
along the wall.

Swinging up.
Swinging high.
Pumping–stretching–
Hello, sky!

Ladder up,
down so fast.
Sliding whoosh.
Daddy? Catch!

Up the hill
to the very top.
Rolling down . . .
I can't stop.

Monkey up,
wiggling toes.
Upside down,
my tummy shows!

Swing me up,
swing me around.
My feet don't want
to touch the ground.

Toss me up!
Toss me high,
so I can spread my wings
and fly-

up as high
as an airplane goes,
clouds and sky
between my toes.

Fly me up,
into a tree.
Come on, Daddy,
sit with me.

Up in a tree,
way up high,
we can almost
touch the sky.

Up in a tree,
I'm safe and snug—
tucked inside
my daddy's hug.